MARVEL STUDIOS

CAPTAIN AMERICA™

T H E   F I R S T   A V E N G E R

OPERATION
SUPER-SOLDIER

Adapted by
Elizabeth Rudnick

Based on the Motion Picture Screenplay by
Christopher Markus & Stephen McFeely

MARVEL
NEW YORK

MARVEL

Published by Marvel Press, an imprint of Disney Book Group. No part of this book may be reproduced or transmitted in any form or by any means, electronic or mechanical, including photocopying, recording, or by any information storage and retrieval system, without written permission from the publisher. For information address Marvel Press, 114 Fifth Avenue, New York, New York 10011-5690.

Printed in the United States of America

First Edition

3 5 7 9 10 8 6 4 2

J689-1817-1-11175

ISBN 978-1-4231-4633-9

ALL OVER AMERICA, men lined up to fulfill the same dream. They wanted to be United States soldiers.

Some were taller, some were shorter. Some were muscular and some were skinny. But as long as these young men received a IA stamp on their recruitment papers, they would fight side-by-side.

Steve Rogers wasn't tall. And he wasn't particularly strong. But he did have a lot of heart, and he wanted to help America.

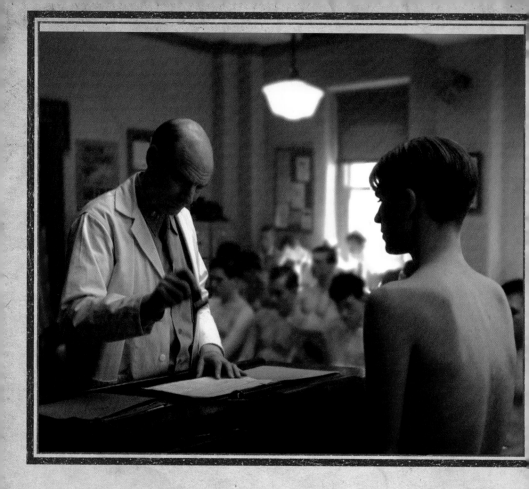

Steve made his way across the recruitment room. The army doctor opened his file. Every ailment had been checked off. The doctor shook his head. "Sorry, son. You'd be ineligible on your asthma alone."

Then he gave Steve a 4F stamp, which meant Steve had failed again.

Later that day, Steve sat in a dark movie theater. On the screen, a newsreel showed footage from the war.

"Let 'em clean up their own mess!" someone in the audience shouted.

Steve couldn't believe his ears. What was this guy's problem? "You want to take it outside, pal," Steve said, turning to face the guy.

Then he gulped. The guy had stood up. And he was very, very big. This was going to get ugly.

In the alley behind the theater, Steve put up his fists. He bobbed and weaved and even managed to get in a solid hit.

But then the other guy picked up Steve and slammed him to the ground. Battered, he got back on his feet and braced himself for another round. Steve grabbed the closest thing he could find—a garbage-can lid—and held it in front of him like a shield. The big guy pulled back his arm and was about to swing . . . when someone grabbed his fist!

"What's with all the fighting?" James "Bucky" Barnes said casually.

Bucky was Steve's best friend. With a swift kick, Bucky sent the other guy running. Then he turned back to help his friend. As he did, he noticed the enlistment form sticking out of Steve's pocket . . . with the 4F stamp on it.

"Tell me you didn't try to enlist again," he said.

Steve shrugged. Bucky didn't understand. And how could he? Bucky was going to war. He was already wearing a uniform and would fly to England the next day. It would be the first time since they were kids that Steve wouldn't be by his side.

Seeing the sad look on his pal's face, Bucky held up the local paper. A headline read: 1942 WORLD EXHIBITION OF TOMORROW. Maybe seeing "the future" would help Steve forget about the present.

Later that night, the two friends stood in the middle of the exhibition. Above them, a monorail

glided silently past while all around, people took in
the sights.

On one stage, a handsome young gentleman
stood by a fancy new Cadillac. A sign read: STARK
STAGE. Steve recognized the man. His name was
Howard Stark, and he was always in the papers
for inventing some new weapon or dating a
beautiful actress.

Something caught Steve's eye and he wandered
away. He wasn't interested in Stark's show. He was
interested in the army-recruitment pavilion nearby.

"You're really going to do this now?" Bucky asked when Steve began to walk away.

Steve nodded. "I'm going to try my luck. This is the war that counts," he said. "And I mean to be counted."

He held out his hand. After a moment, Bucky took it and they shook. This was their good-bye. Tomorrow, Bucky would be fighting for his country. Steve just hoped he'd be close behind.

Turning, Steve entered the recruitment pavilion. An older man stood inside. "So," the

man said in a German accent, "you want to be a fighter, heh?"

"You're with the army?" Steve said, confused by the doctor's accent.

"Doctor Abraham Erskine," the man said, nodding. "Special Scientific Reserve, US Army." The SSR? Steve thought.

He shrugged. A special branch of the army was still the army. Steve gave the doctor his name and waited while he found his file and read through it.

"Five exams in five different cities. All failed,"
the doctor said. "You are very tenacious."

"I don't like bullies, Doc," Steve answered.

Dr. Erskine looked thoughtful. He took in
Steve's small size, his weak muscles—and the
determination in his eyes. "So you would fight,
yes?" Erskine asked.

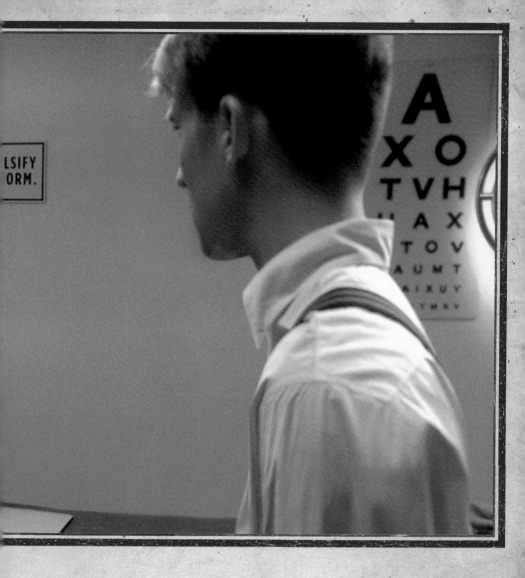

Steve nodded confidently.

As Dr. Erskine laid the file on the table and picked up a stamp, Steve's heart began to race.

"I can offer you a chance," the doctor said. "Only a chance." He brought the stamp down on the file. 1A.

Steve was in!

At a secret military base, Steve and eleven
other recruits stood in formation, waiting to meet
their commanding officers.

They didn't have to wait long. First, a young
woman with a British accent introduced herself
as Agent Peggy Carter. Next up was Colonel
Chester Phillips. He was a tough war veteran with
no sympathy for newbies. Along with Dr. Erskine,
these two would oversee all training. And, they
informed the men, that training would start now!

A short time later, Steve found himself in the middle of an obstacle course. He tripped over a tire and fell face-first. Then he tried to climb a wall and tumbled back down.

"Our goal is to create the finest army in history," Colonel Phillips shouted as he watched the recruits. "Every army starts with one man. By the end of this week, we're going to choose that man."

The colonel turned and gave a pointed look at Steve, as if to say, "but not this one."

Steve gulped and kept running.

The training continued. Steve scrambled up a cargo net and crawled under barbed wire. And the obstacles weren't even the hardest part! Every time he started to make progress, another soldier would step on him or trip him, hoping to make him fail. But Steve kept going. And that didn't go unnoticed.

Dr. Erskine and Peggy watched Steve closely and liked what they saw. He had heart. He would need that for what was to come next.

He was their guy.

That night, Steve sat on his bed in the now-empty barracks. Everyone else had gone home. Hearing the sound of footsteps, he looked up and saw Dr. Erskine walking toward him.

"Why me?" Steve asked when the older man sat down.

The doctor sighed. He told Steve he had not always worked for the SSR. Before, he'd been a scientist working for the enemy. He'd managed to create a special serum that was capable of giving men superhuman powers.

Steve raised an eyebrow. Superhuman powers were just science fiction, he thought. But Dr. Erskine went on.

HYDRA had wanted that power to create an unbeatable army. "One HYDRA agent in particular— Johann Schmidt—grew so obsessed with having such power that he took the serum himself," Dr. Erskine said. "There were . . . complications. The serum amplifies what is inside," Dr. Erskine continued. "Good becomes great, and bad becomes worse. This is why you were chosen. You are not a perfect soldier . . . but a good man."

The next day, Steve was brought to a top secret lab that was hidden deep beneath an antiques shop in Brooklyn, New York. Inside, technicians operated machinery and engineers manned monitors. Up in an observation room, several official-looking men were gathered.

In the middle of all the action was what looked like a large, man-shaped cradle: the Rebirth device.

Steve took a deep breath and stepped inside. There was no turning back now.

As attendants hooked Steve up to various monitors, a man in a suit made adjustments to the device.

"How are your levels, Mr. Stark?" Dr. Erskine asked.

Steve looked over, surprised to see the young inventor in the lab. What did he have to do with SSR?

"We're ready as we'll ever be," Stark answered.

Dr. Erskine and a nurse began to insert six vials full of blue liquid into injectors. Another technician attached pads covered with hundreds of tiny needles to Steve's skin. Then he was strapped down.

"Beginning serum infusion in five, four, three, two . . ." Dr. Erskine counted down. At "one," the doctor threw a switch. The pads pressed down on Steve, emptying the fluid into his body.

As everyone in the room watched, Steve's head shook, and his eyes glowed blue. When the vials were empty, the Rebirth device tilted upright and its panels closed, sealing Steve inside. Only his face could be seen through a small window.

When he was given the signal, Stark threw another switch and turned a dial. Power surged through the device and activated the serum. Ten . . . twenty . . . thirty . . . Steve's eyes squeezed tight . . . fifty . . . sixty . . . the heart-rate monitor began to beep faster and faster . . . a scream echoed over the speakers . . . eighty . . . ninety . . . one hundred . . . and then—silence.

Suddenly, a steady beep . . . beep . . . beep filled the room.

Walking over, Stark carefully opened the device's panels. There was a loud gasp. The scientists and technicians were eager to see if the serum had worked. But even they were surprised by what they saw.

Standing there, amid the smoke and the machines was the new and improved Steve Rogers. Instead of being frail and sickly, Steve had become tall and incredibly muscular.

The experiment had worked!

Steve Rogers's dream had come true. Not only was he in the army, but he was now America's very own Super-Soldier! He would put his new abilities and all of his training to the test on the battlefield. He would save his friends and help the United States win the war.

And he would forever be known throughout the world as CAPTAIN AMERICA!